Meet PJ Robot!

Based on the episode "PJ Robot"

Simon Spotlight
New York   London   Toronto   Sydney   New Delhi

SIMON SPOTLIGHT
An imprint of Simon & Schuster Children's Publishing Division
New York London Toronto Sydney New Delhi
1230 Avenue of the Americas, New York, New York 10020
This Simon Spotlight paperback edition December 2018
This book is based on the TV series PJ MASKS © Frog Box / Entertainment One UK Limited / Walt Disney EMEA Productions Limited 2014;
Les Pyjamasques by Romuald © (2007) Gallimard Jeunesse. All Rights Reserved. This book/publication © Entertainment One UK Limited 2018.
Adapted by Natalie Shaw from the series PJ Masks

SIMON SPOTLIGHT and colophon are registered trademarks of Simon & Schuster, Inc.
For information about special discounts for bulk purchases, please contact Simon & Schuster Special Sales at 1-866-506-1949 or business@simonandschuster.com.
Manufactured in the United States of America 1118 LAK
10 9 8 7 6 5 4 3 2 1
ISBN 978-1-5344-3026-6 (pbk)
ISBN 978-1-5344-3027-3 (eBook)

The PJ Masks are outside Romeo's lab. They can hear Romeo working on something. . . .

"What's he doing this time?" Gekko asks Owlette and Catboy.

Romeo comes out holding a device with buttons and an antenna. "My best invention ever!" Romeo says, thinking he is alone.

The next day Greg, Amaya, and Connor are looking at some things they found near Romeo's lab.

"A screw, a bolt . . . I don't even know what this bit is," Greg says, holding up a piece of metal.

Amaya reminds them that Romeo called it his best invention ever.

"Which means his *horriblest* invention ever," Connor replies.

"Whatever it is, we'll track it down and put it out of action!" adds Greg.

The PJ Masks race out of HQ and head to Romeo's lab. That is when they see a cute, round little robot.

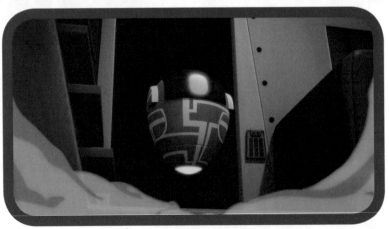

The robot hovers above the ground and circles the PJ Masks before stopping in front of them. It makes beeps and buzzing sounds, and seems to say, "Hello."

"Hello?" Gekko says cautiously. He isn't sure if the robot is friendly.

Then the robot nuzzles Gekko, cuddles up to Owlette, and gives Catboy a hug. Catboy giggles. The robot is so sweet, but Gekko is confused. "Romeo made *this*?" he asks the PJ Masks.

"Why would Romeo invent a robot that's nice?" Owlette asks. "Something's not right. . . ."

Then Catboy hears someone talking. He uses his Super Cat Ears to overhear better. It's Romeo talking about his plan.

"Wait till they totally love it and take it back to HQ!" Romeo says. "Then I'll use the Robot-Controller to make it do what I say."

Soon after, Romeo makes his other robots take the little robot away.

"But . . . it was having fun with us!" Gekko protests.

Romeo says his other robots don't follow orders, so he set up this one with the Robot-Controller. He pushes a button on the controller, and the little robot salutes. When Romeo says "sit," the robot sits. When Romeo says "jump," the robot jumps!

"At last! A robot I can control!" Romeo says.

Suddenly one of Romeo's other robots malfunctions and begins to chase Romeo. Romeo runs away but drops the Robot-Controller! Catboy turns it off so Romeo can't use it to control the little robot anymore.

"How about hanging out with us?" Catboy asks, and the little robot does a happy twirl!

Back at HQ, the little robot helps out. He polishes the Gekko-Mobile at record speed!

Gekko is impressed. "Wow, that's super-lizard-shiny!"

Then Catboy asks the little robot to beam a laser light on the floor, and Catboy chases after it to practice his Super Cat Speed!

Owlette shows the little robot the Picture Player. When he sees a picture of the PJ Masks saving the day, he claps and strikes a PJ Masks pose!

"He doesn't just want to help us," Catboy tells his friends. "He wants to *be* one of us!"

Then the robot brings up a picture of Romeo building a new invention. It seems to be trying to warn them! Gekko tells Owlette and Catboy to look into it. "I'll look after . . . PJ Robot!" he says.

Owlette and Catboy race out of HQ. They spot Romeo and his other robots in the park, building a giant version of the Robot-Controller.

"Wait till this Super Robot-Controller's juiced up!" Romeo tells the robots. "I'll control the little robot again. I'll make it destroy their HQ like I planned!"

When Owlette and Catboy get back to HQ, they find that Gekko has painted PJ Robot in PJ Masks colors. He's now red, green, and blue, just like Owlette, Gekko, and Catboy!

"He loves being here!" Gekko tells them. "He's been using the Picture Player, checking out the vehicles, exploring HQ. . . ."

Owlette is worried. "Exploring HQ? I don't think that's a good idea. What if Romeo gets control of him again?" she asks.

Catboy tells Gekko that Romeo is building a new giant controller!

"When that thing goes on, PJ Robot won't know what he wants. He'll just do what Romeo says . . . and destroy HQ," Owlette warns.

Owlette spots the original controller and has an idea. "What if Romeo does get control of him? We could try and get him back with this!"

Catboy shrugs. "One controller against another is better than nothing," he says.

They race out in the Cat-Car, with PJ Robot by Gekko's side.
"It sure would be good to have PJ Robot on our team," Catboy says.
"Do you really think Romeo can just take him over?" Gekko asks. Then
they see the huge Robot-Controller. "Gasping gekkos, that's BIG!"

The PJ Masks get out of the Cat-Car and tell PJ Robot to stay inside. A light on the giant controller's antenna flashes, and it traps the PJ Masks in a force field. It's not a controller. It's a force-field thrower!

"I knew you'd do *anything* to keep the little robot," Romeo tells the PJ Masks. "I built this *pretend* controller and waited for you to come!"

Romeo finds the original Robot-Controller and pushes a button. It takes control of PJ Robot, and pulls him out of the Cat-Car and toward Romeo!

Gekko shouts, "No, come back! You would've been the best PJ Robot ever! We could have saved the day!"

PJ Robot glows pink . . . and begins to fight back!

PJ Robot breaks free and races over to Romeo's lab, which had been propping up the giant controller. He drives the lab out of the way, and the giant controller falls and breaks. The PJ Masks are freed from the force field, all thanks to PJ Robot!

"Right on, PJ Robot!" Gekko shouts. "So long, Romeo!"

Romeo orders his other robots to attack, but the largest robot sits down, and crosses its arms. "I too do not wish to be controlled. Be nice to me," says the big robot.

Romeo is mad. He is confused, too. "Can I at least make my getaway?" he asks.

"Only if you say 'please,'" the robot insists . . . and this time Romeo follows the robot's orders!

The PJ Masks are ready to celebrate.
"To HQ, everyone!" Owlette says.
"PJ Robot, welcome to the team!" Gekko says.
PJ Robot smiles brightly and strikes his PJ Masks pose!

This time, the PJ Masks—and PJ Robot—save the day together!
Better yet, the PJ Masks have a new friend.

PJ Masks all shout hooray! 'Cause in the night, we saved the day!